I Can Read

Written by Louise A. Gikow

Illustrated by John Patience

My First READER

children's press®

A Division of Scholastic Inc.

New York Toronto London Auckland Sydney

Mexico City New Delhi Hong Kong

Danbury, Connecticut

Library of Congress Cataloging-in-Publication Data

Gikow, Louise.
  I can read / written by Louise A. Gikow ; illustrated by John Patience.
     p. cm. — (My first reader)
  Summary: A child is excited and proud about learning to read.
  ISBN 0-516-24678-X (lib. bdg.)   0-516-25114-7 (pbk.)
  [1. Reading—Fiction. 2. Stories in rhyme.] I. Patience, John, ill. II. Title. III. Series.
  PZ8.3.G376I 2004
  [E]—dc22

                    2004000240

1 2 3 4 5 6 7 8 9 10 R 13 12 11 10 09 08 07 06 05 04

Note to Parents and Teachers

Once a reader can recognize and identify the 44 words used to tell this story, he or she will be able to successfully read the entire book. These 44 words are repeated throughout the story, so that young readers will be able to recognize the words easily and understand their meaning.

The 44 words used in this book are:

all	I'm	pup	too
and	is	rat	toys
are	it	read	true
bat	jam	reading	two
can	jet	see	up
cat	learned	that	what
cup	letter	the	word
grown	letters	then	words
guess	make	there's	yes
hat	mat	this	yet
I	one	three	you

I can read.

Can you read yet?

This word is jam.

That word is jet.

jet

This word is toys.

Pup

That word is pup.

I can read!

17

I'm all grown up.

a b c d e f g
h i j k l m n
o p q r s t u
v w x y z

I learned one letter,
then two, then three.

21

The letters make up words, you see!

There's bat, rat, hat, and mat.

This word is cup. That word is cat.

I can read!

Yes, it is true.

I Can Read

Guess what? You are reading, too!

31

ABOUT THE AUTHOR

Louise A. Gikow has written hundreds of books for children (and a few for young adults and grown-ups, too). She has also written songs and scripts for videos and television shows. Most recently, she was a writer for *Between the Lions,* the PBS-Kids TV series that helps children learn to read. She wanted to write this story because she loves reading more than almost anything (except her family, of course!).

ABOUT THE ILLUSTRATOR

John Patience is the illustrator and author of more than 150 children's books. He works in various styles on a range of books from modern educational to retellings of classic fairy tales. He was born in England and lives with his wife, Jane, and their German shepherd, Layla, in the Yorkshire Dales. He has two grown-up children, Kerry and Joe.